SHADOW SIBLINGS ™

SHADOW SIBLINGS™
DISCOVERING YOUR UNKNOWN SUPERPOWER

WRITTEN BY MOTHER AND DAUGHTER
NICOLE LEINBACH & CLAIRE REYHLE
ILLUSTRATED BY KATIE RUTLEDGE OVERGARD

Printed in the United States of America

First Printing, 2021

ISBN-13: 978-1-939116-00-0 print edition
ISBN-13: 978-1-939116-04-8 ebook edition

Waterside Productions
2055 Oxford Ave
Cardiff, CA 92007
www.waterside.com

To every mom I have ever shared time with.
I'm so grateful for each of you.

And especially to my own mother . . .

Who taught me what love,
grace and strength is truly about.

— **Nicole Leinbach**

To my Oma.
I'll be forever grateful for her love,
support and encouragement.

And to my friends.
Life would be so boring without them!

— **Claire Reyhle**

"I'm so excited to go on vacation," six-year-old Emma exclaimed as she skipped towards the security checkpoint line at her local airport.

"Me, too!" Emma's brother Max shouted as he grabbed his mom's hand and looked ahead at the crowd of people waiting in line.

As Emma and Max anxiously headed towards the long line of people waiting to get through security, Emma couldn't help but notice the many stares she was receiving.

"Mom," Emma whispered as she pulled her mother's coat. "Why are so many people staring at me?"

"Well, sweetie, there are a lot of people here and everyone is just looking around. You are too, right?" Emma's mother replied.

"Yes, Mommy, I am."

"In life, you will see new people, new places, and new things all the time. That's part of what keeps it both exciting and interesting," Emma's mom further explained. "As we go through the airport, I am sure you will better understand what I mean. You should pay attention and let me know what you discover."

As Emma's eyes widened, and she continued through the security line with her brother and parents, she continued to observe a variety of people staring her way. Her brother, however, seemed to be oblivious to the world. As he held his favorite toy and his mother's hand, he took each step ahead with ease and excitement.

As Emma, Max and their parents waited for the airport tram to take them to their terminal, a little boy approached Max and asked him a question.

"Why do you have no hair," he asked.

Max stood there for a second in silence but before he could say a word, Emma chimed in.

"He has alopecia," Emma replied with confidence. "It simply means his body doesn't produce hair the way most people's bodies do, but that's okay."

"Oh," he simply replied. "Okay."

As the little boy walked away, Emma and Max stepped onto the tram and continued their journey through the airport. As they were about to sit on the tram bench, a little boy about Emma's age asked Emma if she could save some space for his sister.

"My sister takes a little longer to walk and would appreciate sitting down. Can you please save her a spot to sit?"

Emma turned her attention to the girl slowly walking towards the tram bench and realized she was using two walking sticks. She recognized that they were different than the crutches she remembered her cousin using once after a sports injury, but wasn't sure what they were called. She then returned her attention to the girl's brother.

"Of course," Emma told the boy as she stood up and made room for the girl to sit down.

Stepping off the tram, Emma couldn't stop thinking about the girl who used two walking sticks to help her get from one spot to another. Her attention was quickly distracted by a young boy, however, who was holding his hands over his ears and shaking side to side as they went down an escalator towards their terminal.

"Mom," Emma said. "Look at him."

"Remember when you said you thought people were staring at you?" Emma's mom asked.

"Yes," Emma replied.

"Well, it's not nice to stare and it's not nice to point, sweetie. It's okay to observe things and recognize what is going on around you, but please try and do so with more compassion."

"Okay, mom."

"But Emma, it is okay that you are curious. That's normal. It looks like he may be uncomfortable with the noise of this very loud airport. Everyone is different, and this may be outside his comfort zone," Emma's mom further explained.

As Emma thought about what her mom said, her eyes continued to look around and explore all the various people at the airport.

Emma's family found their way to their gate, where Emma and Max quickly positioned themselves in seats looking directly out the airport windows.

"Wow, look at how big that plane is!" Max exclaimed.

Emma glanced out the windows, but quickly jumped up from her seat and asked her mom to take her to the bathroom.

As Emma and her mother held hands walking towards the bathroom, Emma noticed a young girl who was bald like her brother. She didn't think much about it, then continued onto the bathroom where they had to wait in a long line.

RESTROOM

Emma impatiently bounced up and down in line as it seemed to take forever to move forward, then finally it was almost her turn. The next bathroom stall to open up was the handicap one, and Emma anxiously ran towards it as soon as its door opened.

"Emma, stop," her mother exclaimed.

"Mom, I have to go!" Emma shouted.

"No, Emma. You need to wait. The handicap stall is for those people who need extra space due to various challenges or disabilities they may have."

Seemingly frustrated, Emma stepped back and waited for the next stall to open.

As Emma and her mother washed their hands, Emma noticed in the bathroom mirror that someone behind her was in a wheelchair. She paused for a moment, watched the woman roll by her, then finished washing her hands. Emma walked towards her mom and looked up to her with sad eyes.

"Mom, I feel bad now," Emma said.

"Why?" Emma's mom asked.

"Well, I just saw a lady in a wheelchair, and I feel bad because she does need extra space to get around. She had to ask people to move just to get her wheelchair through the bathroom," Emma explained. "I understand now why they have special bathroom stalls for people who may need extra room like for those who use wheelchairs."

"You don't need to feel bad, Emma, but I am glad you are beginning to understand. Remember, everyone is different and that's okay. It's just important you respect and understand people's unique differences."

"Mom, let's get some snacks for the plane ride," Emma said as they headed back towards their gate.

"Good idea, Emma. What are you in the mood for?" Emma's mom asked.

"Well, nothing with peanuts because Max is allergic. Let's get pretzels, maybe some gum, and I'd love a juice box, too."

"Perfect," Emma's mom said.

As Emma and her mom walk into the airport gift shop, Emma found her favorite pretzels then looked for juice boxes. She reached up to grab the last two, knowing her brother Max would want one, also.

"Oh, no." Emma heard someone say. As she looked over her shoulder and behind her, she saw a teenage boy. They made eye contact, then he explained to her that he also wanted those same juice boxes.

"My sister has diabetes. We need to make sure she is okay on our flight in case her blood sugar gets low," the boy explained.

Emma didn't understand what that meant, but she did realize it seemed important. She let the boy take the juice boxes, then grabbed two bottles of water instead for her and Max.

As Emma and her mother returned to their boarding gate, Emma thought about all the different kinds of people she saw while walking through the airport. She sat down in a chair next to her brother Max, then told him about one of the people she saw.

"Guess what, Max?" she said.

"What?" he asked.

"I saw another kid with no hair."

"Cool," Max responded with a smirk then looked the other way.

Just then, the attendant at the airport gate announced that boarding was about to begin. But before regular boarding was to take place, pre-boarding would happen.

"That's us!" Max shouted with excitement.

Because of Max's peanut allergy, Emma and her family pre-board planes to wipe down the airplane seats just in case there was peanut dust from past passengers. This helps to ensure more safety for Max due to his peanut allergy.

Joining them in line were a variety of people, including one in a wheelchair, a lady with a walking stick, and another little boy who had a pre-boarding ticket in his hand due to peanut allergies.

Once Emma's mother wiped each of the seats for her family and everyone was settled in, Emma noticed the same bald girl she had seen earlier boarding the plane and pointed her out to her brother.

"Look, Max. There's that girl I told you about. I bet she has alopecia, too."

Just then, Emma's mom turned her attention to the young girl boarding the plane. She could see she looked tired and frail, and that her mother boarding with her also looked a bit exhausted. She also noticed a bag from a local hospital for cancer treatment.

"Sweetie, I don't think that little girl has alopecia. I think she may have cancer." Emma's mom explained.

"Cancer?" Emma replied with surprise. "I thought only older people got that like Grandma did."

"Unfortunately cancer can happen to anyone at any age. Even children can get cancer, and sometimes the medicine they use to try and fight it causes hair loss," Emma's mom explained.

Emma's eyes turned away from her mother and towards Max. She stared at his bald head, then gave him a big hug.

"I'm so glad you have alopecia," Emma told her brother as she squeezed him tight. He pushed her away, then simply replied, "me too."

The plane took off and Max drifted asleep while Emma and her mother chatted about all the different people they saw at the airport.

"Mom," Emma said. "I am really happy I got to see so many different types of people today."

"Why is that?" Emma's mom asked.

"I had no idea there were so many different types of kids with different types of challenges and differences. I guess I never took the time to think about it before."

"You know, Emma, your brother often stands out for being bald and you stand out, too, because you are such a good sister and help others understand that he is okay. He's just different than most kiddos. Today, when you noticed all the other kids who also were a bit different, did you also notice many of them had siblings like you who were helping them?"

Emma shrugged her shoulders then replied, "I guess so."

"Like the boy on the tram who asked you to save a seat for his sister, and the boy who needed the juice boxes for his sister who needed them. They are so lucky to have each other, just like Max is lucky to have you."

Emma thought about what her mom had said. She glanced out the window, then simply replied to her mother, "I'm his shadow sibling."

Emma's mom smiled. She had a feeling she understood what Emma meant, but wanted to hear from Emma firsthand what she thought a shadow sibling was.

"A shadow sibling is the sister or brother of someone who is challenged or different than most kids. The attention is usually on these kids first as a result of their differences. So as their sibling, we live in their shadows, but that's okay. That's where we're meant to be." Emma explained.

Her mother paused for a moment, thought about what Emma had said and then nodded with agreement. She then took her daughter's hand and smiled with pride.

"It's not always easy being in the shadow of your brother or anyone, but it's an important responsibility and one you should be proud of," Emma's mom said.

"I am proud, mom," Emma stated. Then she continued to explain to her mother how she felt.

"Some kids are born to stand out, like Max does. And other kids, like me, shine brightest in their shadows."

"I am so proud of you for recognizing just how important your role is as your brother's shadow sibling. You make me very proud." Emma's mother said as she reached for her daughter's hand and gave her a gentle, loving squeeze.

Emma smiled back at her mother, then stated with confidence and pride, "I'm a shadow sibling. And that's my superpower."

Let's explore what it's like to BE

SHADOW SIBLINGS™

Questions to ask children who are Shadow Siblings:

1. Have you ever recognized the unique role you have as a sibling to someone who needs extra care or gets extra attention?

2. Do you feel as if you get your own extra care or extra attention because you are a Shadow Sibling? Or do you not feel you get any extra care or attention? How does this make you feel?

3. What are some of your favorite memories from being a Shadow Sibling? What have been some more difficult experiences you have had?

4. What types of emotions have you experienced being a Shadow Sibling? Please explain.

5. If you could offer advice to fellow Shadow Siblings, what would you tell them?

Let's explore what it's like to KNOW

SHADOW SIBLINGS™

Questions to ask children who know Shadow Siblings:

1. Do you know anyone who is a Shadow Sibling? If so, who are they? Please tell me about them.

2. Have you ever recognized the unique role that Shadow Siblings have due to their brothers and/or sisters that need extra care or get extra attention due to challenges, circumstances or health conditions that their siblings have?

3. What emotions do you imagine Shadow Siblings experience due to their unique role?

4. If you could offer a Shadow Sibling words of strength, support and encouragement, what would you tell them?

5. If you know a Shadow Sibling, what is one of your favorite memories with this person and why?

MEET THE AUTHORS

Shadow Siblings was inspired by brother and sister duo Claire and Jackson Reyhle along with their mother, Nicole Leinbach.

When Jackson was just three years old, he began to lose his hair to a condition called Alopecia. This unfamiliar and rare autoimmune disease caused a spiral of emotions to follow on top of Jackson losing all his hair from head to toe in response to the most advanced form of Alopecia known as Alopecia Universialis.

In the following years that would pass, Nicole recognized that Alopecia didn't just happen to Jackson. It impacted her daughter, as well, in a way that would forever shape her personality, her responsibilities and her overall perspective and approach to life. As she observed other families with children who had challenges, disabilities or circumstances that made them different, she realized Claire wasn't alone in these emotions or experiences but rather collectively, these children stood together in the shadows of their brothers or sisters. These kids, as Nicole would begin to refer to them, were "shadow siblings".

Claire, Jackson and Nicole live in Denver, Colorado with their extended and blended families. Together they offer inspiration and support to kids born to stand out and those who shine brightest in their shadows through their series of books, merchandise, experiences and more.

Share your own story of being a shadow sibling, get in touch with the Shadow Sibling team, explore Shadow Siblings swag and make connections at ShadowSiblings.com.

Want to support the

SHADOWSIBLINGS™

in your life?

Visit **www.ShadowSiblings.com** to explore
Shadow Siblings Swag, Stories & More!

Made in the USA
Middletown, DE
18 April 2021